Copyright © 2023 Jack Cooper

All rights reserved. No part of this book may be reproduced or transmitted in any form or by any means electronic or mechanical including photocopying, recording, or by any information storage and retrieval system without permission in writing from the publisher or Author.

Aurora Books, an imprint of Eco-Justice Press, L.L.C.

Aurora Books
P.O. Box 5409 Eugene, OR 97405
www.ecojusticepress.com

Silly Lily's Rhyming Adventures in Nature
Written by Jack Cooper
Illustrated by Greta Gonzalez
Edited by Dennis R. Hoerner PhD

www.sillylilysadventures.com

Library of Congress Control Number: 2023945927
ISBN 978-1-945432-61-3

Silly Lily's
Rhyming Adventures in Nature

Written by Jack Cooper
Illustrated by Greta Gonzalez
Edited by Dennis R. Hoerner PhD

Aurora BOOKS

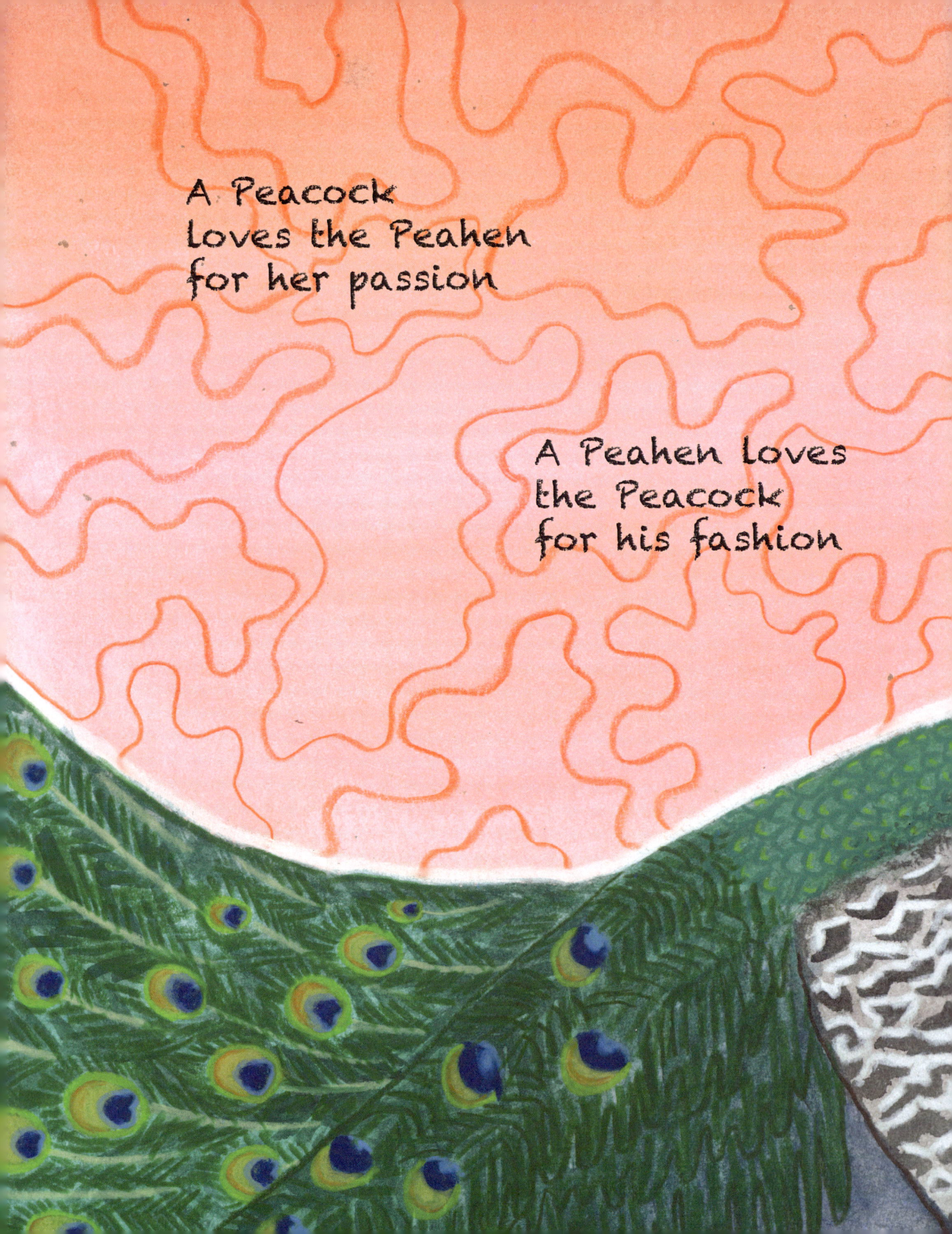

AUTHOR'S NOTE

Silly Lily's Rhyming Adventures in Nature was conceived on a walk through my neighborhood where I noticed a lone rose blooming high above all the leaves in a flower bed. My first thought was, "A rose arose in the rows." Smiling at the play on words, I turned the corner only to see a pair of mallard ducks by the curb nibbling on worms that had wiggled out of the grass during a recent rain. Seeing me, the ducks waddled off to the other side of the street near a drainpipe, and I said out loud, "A duck ducked into a duct," and asked myself, How much fun is this?!

On the way back home, I passed a garden with a statue of a little girl, which I had seen before but never paid much attention to. This day, I noticed she was a fairy with delicate wings and a watering can of flowers. I decided to call her Silly Lily in honor of the two silly rhymes that had just come to me.

As more of these little poems came alive over the next few weeks, they always seemed to be about real plants and animals with real lives, not unicorns or cats in the hat, no Peter Rabbits or Pooh Bears. I wondered if Lily was the source of these puns and homonyms in some magical way, and if there could be a whole children's book of rhymes like these to bring us all closer to the natural world.

My literary friend Dennis Hoerner loved the idea and volunteered to help me, starting by finding an artist who could light up the pages. He contacted his daughter who recommended a gifted high school student named Greta Gonzalez. And so, *Silly Lily's Rhyming Adventures in Nature* arose, just like that garden rose did, through Greta's magical artwork, Dennis's wise counsel and publisher David Diethelm's experienced touch. This book is for the fairy child in all of us.

Jack Cooper

JACK COOPER is the author of the poetry collection Across My Silence (World Audience, Inc., 2007). His work has appeared in numerous publications, including *Earth Island Journal, Rattle* and *North American Review*. His poetry has been nominated four times for a Pushcart Prize and was recently anthologized in *Earth Song: A Nature Poem Experience* (T. S. Poetry Press, NY, 2022). Cooper graduated with a BS in Biology from the University of Redlands, received a second bachelors in English from the University of Trondheim, Norway, and holds a teaching credential from Cal State Dominquez Hills. He is the former communication director at the High Desert Museum in Bend, Oregon, and worked for many years in the same capacity at John Tracy School for Deaf Children in Los Angeles. He lives with his wife Kazuko in Eugene, Oregon. They have a garden with English peas and roses, a cat named CouCou and two sons, Jesse and Clay, in Los Angeles.

GRETA GONZALEZ is an independent artist who grew up in Corvallis, Oregon and starts her first year at Centre College in Danville, Kentucky. She spends her time reading, hiking and playing with her younger siblings. Largely self-taught, she has had a passion for art her entire life, fostered by her elementary education at the Corvallis Waldorf School. In 2022, she attended the selective Governor's School for the Arts in Kentucky. In 2023, her art received an Honorable Mention in the Regional Scholastic Art & Writing Awards. Gonzalez's introduction into the world of illustration began with a recent project for the Letitia Carson Foundation, illustrating a children's book for a local elementary school. Now, she makes her professional debut as illustrator of Silly Lily's Rhyming Adventures in Nature.

DENNIS R. HOERNER PhD specialized in Literature and Psychology. He has taught at several colleges in the U.S. and was a Visiting Professor at Kanazawa National University in Kanazawa, Japan. In 1998 he put his roots down in Eugene, Oregon, where he was the Head of School at a small, non-profit, alternative high school until his recent retirement. Nurturing has been the common theme of his life–in education, psychological counseling, organic gardening, and raising children. A single dad for many years, he always took time to read books to his four kids. His 18-year-old black cat named Tipsy recently died and now joins the forever-loved under a hydrangea in his garden.

A PAGE FOR YOU

Printed in the USA
CPSIA information can be obtained
at www.ICGtesting.com
LVRC090747311223
767725LV00039B/97